Earth's Changing Deserts

by Neil Morris

Raintree

Chicago, Illinois

Printed and bound in China by South China Printing Company
07 06 05 04 03
10 9 8 7 6 5 4 3 2 1

Editorial: Keith Ulrich
Design: Erica Barraca
Picture Services: Michelle Lisseter and Bridge Creative Ltd
Illustrations: Bridge Creative Services Ltd
Production: Sal D'Amico

Cover photograph of a camel caravan in the Takla Makan Desert reproduced with permission of Corbis (Keren Su).

The publishers would like to thank Margaret Mackintosh for her assistance in the preparation of this book.

Library of Congress Cataloging-in-Publication Data

Morris, Neil, 1946-
  Earth's changing deserts / Neil Morris.
    p. cm. -- (Landscapes and people)
Summary: Examines how deserts are formed and how they are constantly changing, what animals and plants live there, ways in which humans live in and change deserts.
Includes bibliographical references and index.
ISBN 1-4109-0176-9 (hc), 1-4109-0343-5 (pb)
1. Deserts--Juvenile literature. 2. Landscape changes--Juvenile literature. 3. Desert ecology--Juvenile literature. [1. Deserts. 2. Desert ecology. 3. Landscape changes. 4. Ecology.] I. Title. II. Series: Morris, Neil, ≠d 1946-   Landscapes and people.
GB612.M676 2003
910'.915'4--dc21

                                    2003006016

Acknowledgments
The publishers would like to thank the following for permission to reproduce photographs:
p. **4** P. Kaya/Bruce Coleman Collection, p. **11** Natural Selection Inc./Bruce Coleman Collection, p. **14** Granville Harris/Bruce Coleman Collection; p. **19** Penny Tweedie/ Corbis,p. **20** Robert van der Hilst/ Corbis, p. **21** Buddy Mays/ Corbis, p. **22**, **28** Carl & Ann Purcell/ Corbis; p. 27 Stone/Getty Images; p. 7 Anthony Bannister/NHPA, p. **13** Daniel Heuclin/NHPA, p. **17** Daniel Heuclin/NHPA, p. **23** Kevin Schafer/NHPA, p. **25** Nigel J. Dennis/NHPA; p. **10** Richard Packwood/Oxford Scientific Films, p. **15** Deni Brown/Oxford Scientific Films, p. **16** Eyal Bartov/Oxford Scientific Films, p. **29** Doug Allan/Oxford Scientific Films; p. 26 Jorgen Schytte/Still Pictures.

Contents

Any words appearing in the text in bold, **like this,**
are explained in the Glossary.

What Is a Desert?

What do you think of when you think of a desert? Is it a very hot place, with **sand dunes** as far as the eye can see? Or is it a flat wilderness where the dry ground is covered in rocks and stones? Whichever one you think of, you're right. A desert can be both of these things, and others, too.

A desert is an area of very dry land that receives very little rain. In fact, deserts receive less than 10 inches (25 centimeters) of rain in a whole year. This means that the ground is dry nearly all the time. Most places in the world have much more rainfall. London, for example, receives about 23 inches (60 centimeters) of rain every year. New York has about 43 inches (110 centimeters), and Sydney, Australia, has about 47 inches (120 centimeters).

∧ *These huge sand dunes dwarf a four-wheel-drive vehicle as it crosses the Sahara Desert in Algeria.*

The biggest desert in the world, the Sahara in Africa, is very hot. The daytime summer temperature is usually around 90°F (32 °C). There are different desert **landscapes,** though. Some deserts, such as the Gobi Desert in Asia, are much cooler for most of the year. The summer temperature in the Gobi Desert is about 70°F (21 °C), but in winter the daytime temperature drops to 10°F (–12 °C).

The icy **polar** regions of Earth are desert regions, too, and the temperatures there are very low. In Antarctica, where the ground is frozen for most of the year, the summer temperature varies between 5°F (–15 °C) and 31°F (–35 °C).

World of deserts

There are big deserts on six **continents** of the world—Africa, Antarctica, Asia, Australia, North America, and South America. Smaller areas of very dry land are also found on the seventh continent, Europe, especially in southern Spain.

Looking at deserts

Earth's deserts formed and spread over millions of years. Since then, they have been constantly changing. They are home to many different kinds of plants and animals that have **adapted** to a difficult life with little water. People, too, have tried to control the deserts for living and farming, and we continue to change them.

⋂ *Hot deserts are found in two bands that stretch around the world. The bands are near the **tropics,** which are Earth's hottest regions. Cooler deserts are farther from the **equator**. The coldest desert is on the frozen continent of Antarctica.*

7

12   14   16

1

2

1 Great Basin   3
2 Sonoran
3 Chihuahua
4 Sechura
5 Atacama
6 Patagonia
7 Greenland (polar desert)
8 Namib
9 Sahara   4
10 Kalahari
11 Arabian
12 Kara–Kum
13 Thar
14 Takla Makan
15 Antarctica (polar desert)
16 Gobi
17 Great Sandy

13

tropic of Cancer

9   11

equator

10   tropic of Capricorn

5   8   17

6

0   3000   6000 miles
0   3000   6000 kilometers

15

N

How Are Deserts Formed?

Water changes in the air, making clouds and then rain. First, the sun heats water on land and in the oceans. The heated water then changes into a gas called water vapor, which rises into the air. As the vapor cools it forms droplets of water, which join together to form clouds. Eventually the water falls back to Earth as rain, snow, sleet, or hail. These are all different forms of **precipitation.**

Deserts are formed by a lack of precipitation. There are various reasons why a particular region has little rainfall and so is very dry. Most deserts are found in the **tropical** regions just to the north and south of the **equator.** As masses of air move toward the equator, they heat up and rise high into the sky. The masses of air are huge and constantly moving. Then the air cools, forms clouds, and drops rain over regions where tropical **rain forests** grow. By the time masses of air reach the lines of the **tropics** (see page 5), they are dry again. The air drops down, and dry winds blow across the regions where deserts are found. There the skies are cloudless and clear, so the sun heats up the ground very quickly.

> The trade winds push air toward the equator, where it heats up, rises, and moves toward the tropics. Many deserts are near the **latitudes** of the tropics.

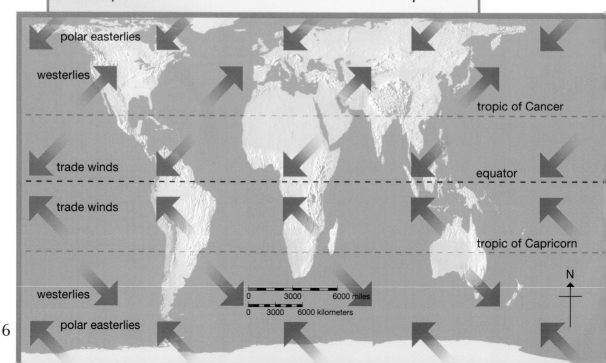

polar easterlies

westerlies

tropic of Cancer

trade winds

equator

trade winds

tropic of Capricorn

westerlies

N

0   3000   6000 miles

0   3000   6000 kilometers

polar easterlies

Mist rolling in from the Atlantic Ocean covers this coastal region of the Namib Desert in southern Africa.

Far from the sea

Other areas become deserts because they are so far from the ocean. The winds that blow inland from the ocean have dropped their rain by the time they reach the middle of a **continent.** The Gobi Desert, in the middle of Asia, is an example. It is so far inland that the winds lose all their **moisture** before they get there.

Along the coast

Some deserts, such as the Atacama in South America, form along the coast. In these regions the seas have cold **currents,** which means the air does not take up much moisture and the winds blowing off the seas are cool and dry. This helps to make deserts. Mist often forms over these coastal deserts, but the ground remains dry. Summer temperatures are generally around 64°F (18 °C) in the Atacama Desert.

In the rain shadow

Some areas become deserts because they are on the sheltered side, or rain shadow, of high mountains. As clouds rise to pass over the mountains, they cool down and drop rain on the slopes below. When the winds reach the other side, they have lost their moisture and are dry.

At night

Deserts are cold places at night. This is because there is no cloud cover. In wetter regions, clouds act like a blanket and keep in the warmth at night. In the desert, though, the temperature may drop by 85°F (30°C) when the sun goes down.

Changing Landscapes

There are many different desert **landscapes**. Some deserts are rocky, others are stony, and some of the most famous deserts are sandy. These sandy deserts are also called **ergs** (from an Arabic word for "area of sand"). But where does the sand come from? It comes from rocks, and it forms over millions of years. As rocks are heated rapidly by the sun during the day, they expand (or get bigger). Then as they cool quickly at night, the rocks contract (get smaller). This causes them to crack. Gradually the rocks begin to crumble into smaller stones and then eventually into tiny grains of sand.

The Arabian Desert covers parts of nine countries and has three main regions. The Syrian Desert is mainly made up of a stony plain. The An Nafud and Rub al-Khali are huge areas of sand dunes (see page 9).

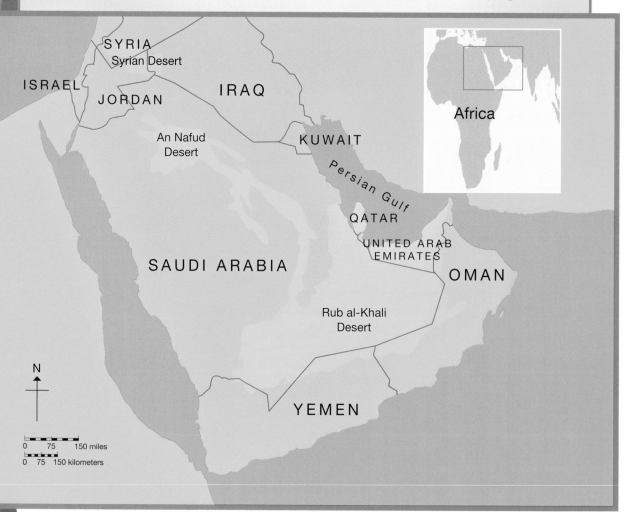

Sand on the move

Like waves on the sea, **sand dunes** are shaped by the wind. They cover up to a quarter of the world's desert areas. Sand dunes move and change shape constantly as winds blow the sand around. Many dunes form around obstacles, such as a rocks, plants, or even dead animals. These obstacles slow the wind down and make it drop any sand it is carrying. The strength and direction of the wind, as well as the nature of the obstacle, affect the shape of the dunes (see the different kinds, below). Most dunes are between 16 and 165 feet (5 and 50 meters) high, but some are much larger. Seif dunes can be 650 feet (200 meters) high and are often many miles long.

(a) Crescent-shaped barchan dunes often form around a boulder. Their "horns" point downwind. (b) Seif dunes (from the Arabic for "sword") are long, parallel ridges. They are often formed when the wind comes from two slightly different directions. (c) Star dunes form when winds blow from many different directions. Their arms stretch out from a central peak.

The empty quarter

The largest sandy region in the world is in the southeastern region of the Arabian Peninsula. The Rub al-Khali Desert is mainly in Saudi Arabia, crossing the border into Yemen, Oman, and the United Arab Emirates. Rub al-Khali means "empty quarter." It is called this because the area is so hot and dry that very few people ever go into this wilderness, and there are few animals and plants there. Even though it is "empty," the region never remains exactly the same. Strong winds constantly blow the sand around, driving it into ripples and waves.

Dawn is breaking over these rocky peaks of the Ahaggar Mountains, in the Algerian Sahara. The highest peak reaches 9,573 feet (2,918 meters).

Rocky uplands and stony plains

The world's rocky deserts are very hot and dry. Rocky uplands are known as **hamadas.** Some rocky deserts have high peaks. Lower, stony plains are called **regs.** Like **erg** (see page 8), "hamada" and "reg" both come from Arabic words. The world's largest desert, the Sahara, has all of these different desert types.

The Sahara

The Sahara (from an Arabic word for "desert") stretches over 3,125 miles (5,000 kilometers) from the Atlantic Ocean to the Red Sea. It covers more than a quarter of the **continent** of Africa and is part of the **landscape** of ten countries. The area of the Sahara is larger than Australia, and not much smaller than the United States! The Sahara has many **sand dunes,** but they cover only about one-fifth of the desert. Most of the Sahara is made up of hamadas. At the Sahara's highest point, in Chad, the Tibesti Mountains rise to 11,204 feet (3,415 meters).

Death Valley

The **barren** lands of California's Death Valley were given their name in 1849. Many **pioneer** families set out from Utah, looking for a better life, and gold, in California. Many failed to make it across the hot, bare valley. Among those who survived, one pioneer is supposed to have said, "Good bye, Death Valley," and the name stuck. Much of the valley is made up of rock, but sand is also blown into dunes. This is the hottest, driest, and lowest place in North America. At one point, near a place called Badwater, the valley is 282 feet (86 meters) below sea level.

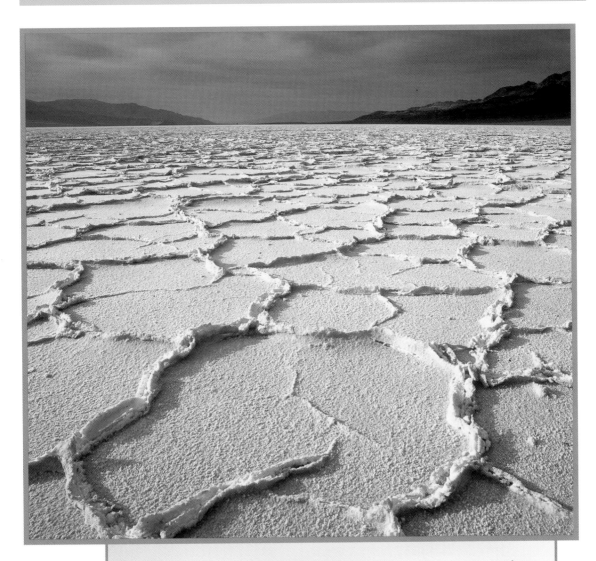

*Death Valley is about 140 miles (225 kilometers) long and 5 to 15 miles (8 to 24 kilometers) wide. Many thousands of years ago, there was a lake in the valley. All that is left of it now are dry **salt flats.***

Mesas and buttes

Wind, sand, and water all play their part in wearing away land in deserts. This process, called **erosion,** makes many of the common shapes seen in dry **landscapes.** Over thousands and millions of years, rivers can carve out huge **canyons,** or gorges, such as the Grand Canyon in Arizona. The canyons divide high **plateaux,** which often wear away to leave flat-topped, steep-sided areas of highland called **mesas.** When a mesa continues to be worn away over many years by storms and winds, separate mounds of rock are left. These smaller features are called **buttes.** Mesas and buttes are common in North American desert regions, such as Monument Valley on the Arizona-Utah border.

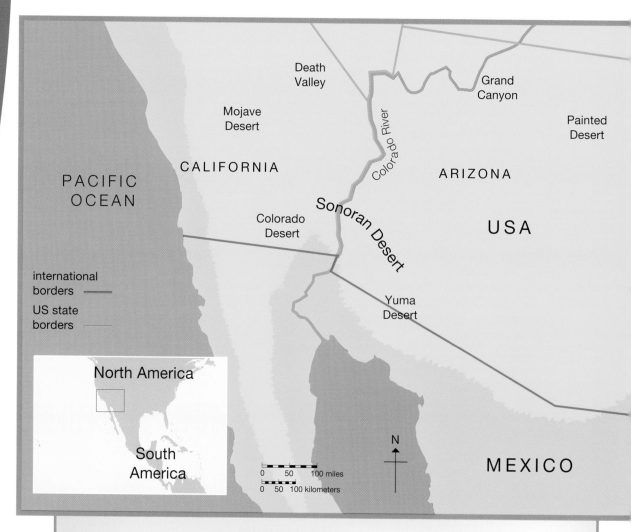

There are many desert regions in the southwestern United States. The largest of them, the Sonoran Desert, covers parts of two states, California and Arizona, as well as parts of northern Mexico.

Rock pinnacles and pedestals

When buttes and single rocks are left standing in the desert, they are gradually worn away even more by fierce winds. These winds carry tiny pieces of stone and sand, which speed along close to the ground. They chip and **scour** away at the rocks, like a sandblasting machine, turning them into thin **pinnacles.** Because of this, the lower parts of tall rocks are worn away more quickly, so they eventually form a mushroom shape. We call these desert rocks **pedestals.**

Sudden floods

Dried-out river beds, called **wadis,** are found in many deserts. They form dry valleys and ravines. Some may have been created many thousands of years ago when their particular region was receiving much more rain. Today, when rare rainstorms do occur, water quickly rushes down the wadis and floods the land. The rushing water carries rocks, stones, and sand, which scour the wadis and make them even deeper. The wadi below, at the edge of the Sahara Desert in Morocco, has not completely dried out. On flat land, shallow lakes are sometimes left after a heavy storm. These lakes, called playas, then dry out in the sun and leave a white layer of salt behind. This happens in Death Valley, California (see page 11).

Changing Life

Deserts are harsh places to live in. The plants and animals that manage to survive have to make do with little water and put up with tremendous changes in temperature. Some plant **species** have changed and **adapted** over thousands of years to cope with desert conditions.

Finding and storing water

Desert plants have to find, collect, and store the little water that is available to them. Cacti are very good at this. They store water in their fleshy stems. The stems are shaped so that any rain flows directly to their roots. They spread their roots out wide, so that they can gather **moisture** before it sinks far into the ground. Cacti are covered with sharp spines. These protect them from thirsty animals, which would otherwise feast on their store of water.

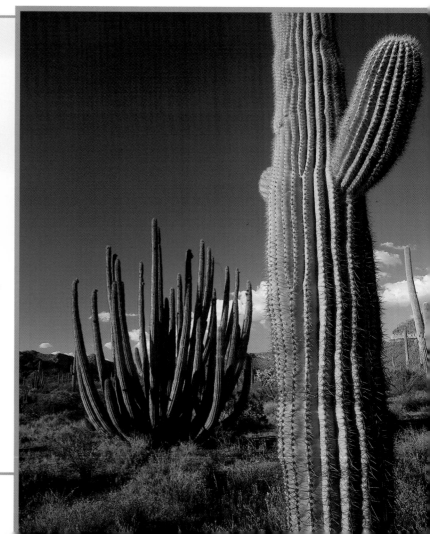

∩ *The giant saguaro of the Sonoran Desert is the tallest cactus in the world. It can grow to a height of up to 55 feet (17 meters). Despite its spines, the saguaro is useful to certain birds. Gila woodpeckers peck their way into the thick stem to make their nests. When they leave, tiny elf-owls take their turns in the ready-made holes. The plant on the left with many stems is called an organ-pipe cactus.*

Adapting to desert life

Some plants have specially adapted to life in the desert. The welwitschia plant of the Namib Desert, in southwest Africa, has adapted so well that it can live for more than a thousand years. It has two long leaves and a 10-foot (3-meter) -long root. The welwitschia takes in moisture from fog and **dew** through millions of **pores** in its leaves, and it stores the water in its root. Other desert plants have a very short life. Whenever it rains, they suddenly shoot up and flower within a few weeks. They scatter their seeds before they die. The seeds have a thick coating that protects them through long periods of **drought.** When rain falls, the coating is washed off and the seeds start to sprout.

These date palms in the Tunisian Sahara can grow up to 98 feet (30 meters) tall.

Providing food and shelter

Desert plants provide animals with food and shelter. One plant is particularly important to desert people: the **date palm.** In the Sahara and Arabian deserts, date palms grow in **oases,** which are small areas where there is water. Dates, the fruit of the palm, provide food for people and animals. Date stones can be ground up to make camel food. Palm leaves are used to thatch roofs for huts or to burn as fuel. **Fibers** from dried palm leaves are twisted into ropes. At the same time, the palms provide shade for other plants, such as small fruit trees.

Protection from heat

Most desert animals avoid the fierce daytime heat by sleeping in cool, dark burrows during the day. They are nocturnal animals, coming out to feed only at night. The desert tortoise does this in the dry regions of Mexico and the United States. Some animals, such as the spadefoot toad, bury themselves and go into a long sleep during the hottest and driest parts of the year. This process is called estivation. When it rains, they quickly wake up and come to the surface again.

Keeping cool

Many reptiles, such as lizards and snakes, are at home in the desert. They are cold-blooded animals and so need heat from the Sun to warm their bodies. They are usually on the move just after sunrise and before sunset, when the desert floor is warm.

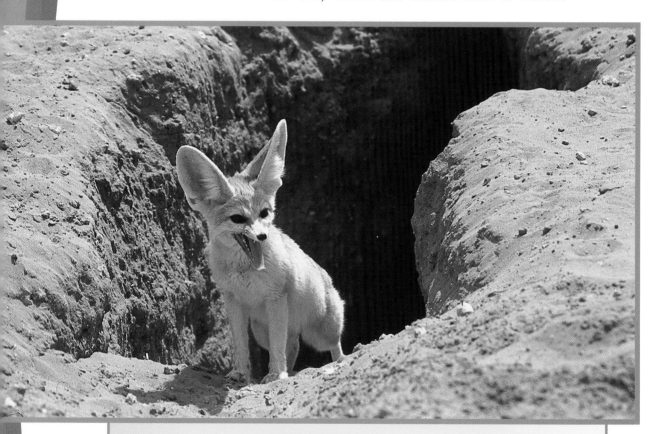

The fennec fox, which lives in the deserts of Africa and Arabia, is the world's smallest fox, but it has the biggest ears. This means it never gets too hot because its large ears help it to lose heat quickly.

Finding water

Desert animals have to survive on very little water. Some insects have **adapted** well to life in the hot desert. Their bodies are covered by tough shells that are coated with wax. The darkling beetle of southern Africa lets **moisture** from morning mist collect on its shiny body. Then it tips itself up to let the water droplets run down to its mouth. Many larger animals manage to survive on the moisture they take in from the blood of their **prey.**

Predators and prey

There are a few large meat-eating animals in the desert. They are **predators,** and their victims are their prey. The predators include members of the cat family, such as the puma in North America. Members of the dog family include the dingo in Australia. The cats and dogs mainly hunt small rodents such as kangaroo rats.

The ship of the desert

The camel is well suited to life in the desert. On its back it has a hump (some have two), in which it stores fat. This acts as a food store and allows camels to go for many days without food or even water. Camels can carry loads for long distances and so have become known as the "ships of the desert." Camels also provide meat, milk, and fleece for desert people.

Changing Settlements

When early humans spread around the world, they hunted wild animals and gathered roots and berries for food as they went. This was never easy in desert regions, so you might think that people would not want to live there. It is certainly true that fewer people live in deserts than in other parts of the world, but certain groups of people **adapted** well to desert life in ancient times. These people did not settle anywhere permanently. They were **nomads** and wandered from place to place to find food.

The Bedouin

Some of the nomadic Bedouin people of Arabia and the Sahara still follow the traditional ways of their ancient **ancestors.** They move around the desert looking for new grazing for their herds of camels, sheep, and goats. They often travel at night, when it is cool, and rest during the heat of the day. Families live together in tents made of woven goat hair.

The yellow area, including the Kalahari Desert, shows the region of southern Africa in which the San people (see page 19) live today. This region spreads across different countries and includes several national parks and reserves, where animals and plants are protected.

San Bushmen

The San people, or Bushmen, of the Kalahari Desert are also nomadic **hunter-gatherers.** Their traditional ways have made them expert at desert survival. The men are skillful hunters, using arrows tipped with poison made from certain beetles. San women and children spend much of their time gathering roots, fruits, and berries. They even get water from the desert by sticking hollow reeds in the dry ground and sucking up underground **moisture.** Their dome-shaped shelters are made from branches thatched with dry grasses. The San people's way of life is changing fast. Once they spread across much of southern Africa, but today there are just a few thousand Sans still living a nomadic life in the desert.

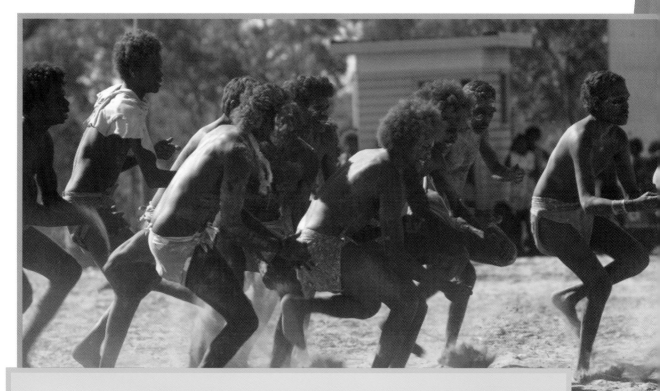

The first Australians

The Aborigines had been living in Australia for tens of thousands of years before settlers arrived from Europe just a few hundred years ago. Over that long period of time, the Aborigines learned how to survive in the dry conditions of their **continent,** which is mostly desert. They hunted kangaroos and other animals with spears and hunting weapons called **boomerangs,** as well as gathering roots and grubs to eat. This traditional way of life was threatened by the European newcomers, but in recent years some parts of the desert have been set aside as protected areas for Aborigines.

Trade routes

In order to be able to cross deserts safely and easily, ancient **merchants** used special routes. They made stops at **oases** on the way, and these developed into settlements. Traders journeyed many hundreds of miles to trading posts such as Mecca (which is now a major city in Saudi Arabia). The route was mostly made up of dusty desert tracks, and camels were the best method of transport. Special stopping places for **caravans** of traders, known as caravanseries, grew up along the trade routes.

Taklimakan Desert

The name of the Chinese desert of Taklimakan means "go in and you won't come out again." This shows what ancient people thought of it, but still they traveled around its edges. They followed the Silk Road, an ancient trade route used by merchants to take silk from China to Europe. When the famous Italian explorer Marco Polo traveled that way in the late 1200s, he put up a sign every night that pointed in the direction his expedition was traveling. The next morning, when the desert all around them looked the same, they knew which way to go.

⌒ *These ruins at the northern edge of the Taklimakan Desert are all that remain of the town of Gaochang. The town was once an important stop on the ancient trade route.*

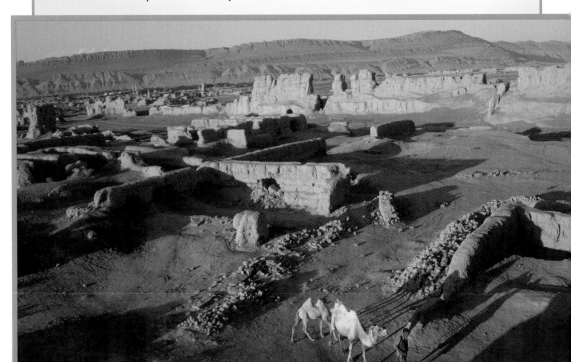

Oasis city

Kashi, at the western edge of the Taklimakan Desert, grew up around an oasis. It became an important stopping place on the Silk Road and was fought over by many different people. Today, the region around the oasis city is still desert, but Kashi is **fertile.** Wheat, maize (corn), and rice are grown there, as well as melons, grapes, and peaches. Today the city has a population of 170,000.

Phoenix, Arizona

Around 1300 c.e. Native Americans of the Hohokam culture dug canals next to a river running through the desert. In this way they were able to **irrigate** the land for farming. In 1867, the abandoned canals were found, and a village began to develop. As it grew, the community was named Phoenix, after a legendary bird that rose from its own ashes. In 1889, Phoenix, at the north edge of the Sonoran Desert, became the state capital of Arizona. By 1950, it had a population of 100,000. Phoenix receives just 8 inches (20 centimeters) of rain each year, however, which means that water is in short supply. Today, almost a million people live in the desert city of Phoenix (above).

Mineral wealth

Gold, silver, diamonds, and other valuable **minerals** are mined beneath the surface of many of the world's hot deserts. Governments often allow companies to develop mines in desert regions, because fewer people live there and so the industry has less of an effect on people's lives. Gold has been mined from Australian deserts for about 150 years. Australia is the third biggest producer of gold in the world (after South Africa and the United States), and is rich in many other minerals, too.

This map shows the major oil fields of the Arabian Peninsula, as well as neighboring Iran. The oil is processed at refineries on the coast of the Persian Gulf, before being poured into tankers and sent to all parts of the world.

Oil Fields
Oil Refineries

0   75   150 Miles
0   75   150 Kilometers

Namibian treasures

The Namib Desert runs in a long strip along the Atlantic coast of Namibia, in southern Africa. Namibia's greatest treasure is its minerals, and many of them come from the desert. The main minerals are diamonds, uranium, copper, lead, and zinc. These also form the country's greatest **exports.** Many are shipped from the deep-water port of Walvis Bay, which is in a small **fertile** region between two strips of desert.

Oil beneath the sands

During the 20th century, oil became one of the most important natural resources in the world. It is used to power factories and cars and to make plastics and many other products. Oil was discovered beneath the Arabian Desert in the 1930s. The discovery brought wealth and many changes to the countries in the region. The largest of these, Saudi Arabia, is the world's leading producer of crude oil. This "black gold" is mined in the desert, then pumped through pipelines to the Persian Gulf coast. There it is put in tankers, which sail around the world.

Solar and wind power

Solar panels can be used to collect the Sun's energy and turn it into electricity. Hot deserts are ideal places to collect solar energy. One of the world's biggest solar-power plants is in the Mojave Desert, California (see below). It generates huge amounts of electricity. **Wind turbines** are also being placed in windy desert regions to create electricity. This can be an ideal location for wind farms, because in other places local people often say that large turbines ruin the view.

Changing Deserts

Many of the world's deserts were formed during the last few thousand years. During this time the world's **climate** has generally changed from cool and wet to more warm and dry. Many deserts are still expanding. The process by which dry regions grow bigger, spread, and become deserts is called desertification.

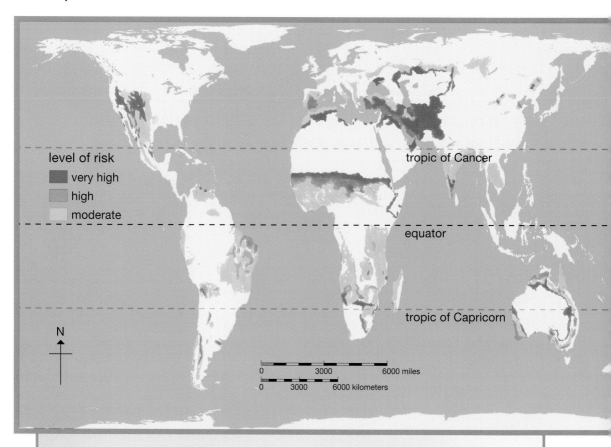

level of risk

- very high
- high
- moderate

tropic of Cancer

equator

tropic of Capricorn

N

0   3000   6000 miles
0   3000   6000 kilometers

∩ *This map shows the areas of the world that are most at risk from desertification. The highest risk is in the countries of central Africa, at the southern edge of the Sahara Desert.*

Climate change

The world's climate is continuing to change, and the overall temperature is still going up slightly. Many scientists believe that this is caused partly by the greenhouse effect, which is created by heat-trapping gases. These gases allow heat through to Earth from the Sun, but they trap it there, like the glass of a greenhouse.

The gases released by burning fuel, such as the exhaust fumes given off by cars, add to this effect. It may cause a general increase in temperature called global warming. This will make the land drier and add to the problems of desertification.

Increasing numbers

As the world's population increases, there are more people trying to make a living at the edge of desert regions. Many of them graze their animals on land that is already at risk. This is happening in the Sahel, a semiarid ("half dry") region that stretches across the south of the Sahara Desert. Cattle and goats are reared there, but a series of terrible **droughts** in the 1970s and 1980s turned much of the land into desert. In Niger (one of the countries of the Sahel), it has been estimated that more than one-third of the population of 10 million are affected by the spreading desert.

This goat herd finds little to eat on dry land near the Kalahari Desert in southern Africa. Eating the little that is left, herds can turn land into desert quickly.

The Dust Bowl

During the 1930s bad droughts turned a region of the southern Great Plains of the United States into a so-called Dust Bowl. Terrible dust storms forced many people to leave the area around western Oklahoma and northern Texas. The region's soil had become dry and loose after its natural grassland was planted with wheat earlier in the century. The soil simply blew away and left a desert area behind.

Fighting the desert

In the United States, the Soil Conservation Service was set up in 1935 to teach farmers how to protect their soil after the terrible dust storms. One of the main methods was to plant large rows of trees. These help reduce the effect of winds at ground level by getting in their way and breaking up their force. Less powerful winds mean that soil and smaller plants are not blown away.

These people in Mauritania, to the west of the Sahara Desert, are putting up brushwood fences. These help stop sand dunes from spreading.

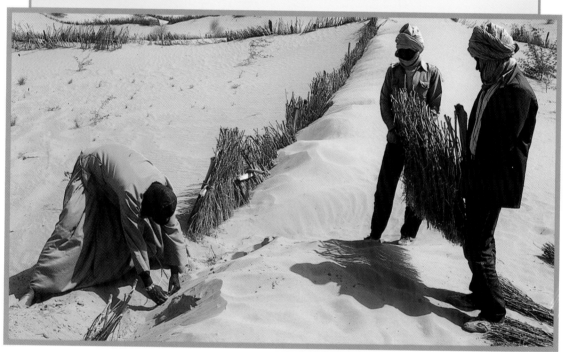

Controlling rivers

The most obvious way to stop land from becoming desert is to **irrigate** it. In many regions, rivers have been dammed so that people can use water to irrigate their land, but this can bring problems, too. In Egypt, where the Nile River flows through the desert at the edge of the Sahara, the annual flood was essential to ancient civilizations. It spread rich, **fertile** mud over farming land. Modern Egyptians wanted more control over the river's waters, and the Aswan High Dam was opened in 1971. This dam stops mud from moving downstream, though, so farmers have to use more chemicals to replace the mud's nutrients and fertilize their land.

Tourism

The world's deserts have become popular with tourists. In North Africa, many visitors take camel rides into the edges of the Sahara. Such activities as these bring money to local people, which can help them keep their environment as it is.

Looking to the future

Deserts are interesting features of Earth's **landscape.** As we have seen, they are much more than **barren** wildernesses. Nevertheless, the desert is a difficult environment in which to live. If deserts were to keep on growing, the loss of farmland could lead to **famine** for many of the world's people. As Earth's **climate** changes, and if its population continues to grow, we will have to make sure that we use land very carefully.

Palm Springs

The popular U.S. resort of Palm Springs, in southern California, lies in a valley of the Colorado Desert. It got its name from the hot springs of the region, but the water from these were not enough to water the desert. This was achieved with water supplied through canals from the nearby Colorado River. Over the last 50 years, Palm Springs has developed into a large, desert tourist resort. The photo (right) shows part of the Desert Princess golf course at Palm Springs. It takes a lot of water to keep the course this green.

Desert Facts and Figures

The world's biggest deserts

desert	continent	area in sq miles	area in sq km
Sahara	Africa	3,243,300	8,400,000
Australian	Australia	598,500	1,550,000
Arabian	Asia	501,900	1,300,000
Gobi	Asia	401,500	1,040,000
Kalahari	Africa	200,800	520,000
Taklimakan	Asia	123,500	320,000
Sonoran	North America	119,700	310,000
Namib	Africa	115,800	300,000
Kara Kum	Asia	104,200	270,000
Thar	Asia	100,400	260,000
Somali Desert	Africa	96,500	250,000
Atacama Desert	South America	69,500	180,000

The world's driest inhabited places

location	country	annual rainfall in in/mm
Aswan	Egypt	0.02 / 0.5
Luxor	Egypt	0.03 / 0.7
Arica	Chile	0.04 / 1.1
Ica	Peru	0.09 / 2.3
Antofagasta	Chile	0.19 / 4.9
Minya	Egypt	0.2 / 5.1
Asyut	Egypt	0.2 / 5.2
Callao	Peru	0.5 / 12
Trujilo	Peru	0.6 / 14
Fayyum	Egypt	0.7 / 19

This ancient Egyptian temple is on the opposite bank of the Nile from Luxor. It is one of the world's driest places.

Polar Deserts

The Antarctic ice sheet is the world's biggest polar desert, measuring 4,839,790 square miles (12,535,000 square kilometers). A polar desert is an area where the annual rainfall is less than 10 inches (250 millimeters), and the average temperature for the warmest month is less than 50°F (10°C). The Greenland ice sheet is also a polar desert, and it measures 666,412 square miles (1,726,000 square kilometers).

> The **continent** of Antarctica, around the South Pole, is the world's biggest ice desert. This is the coldest and windiest place on Earth.

Countries of the Sahara Desert

country	approx. desert area in sq miles	approx. desert area in sq km
Algeria	696,100	1,803,000
Libya	564,500	1,462,000
Sudan	455,200	1,179,000
Niger	397,300	1,029,000
Egypt	339,000	878,000
Mali	291,500	755,000
Chad	233,200	604,000
Mauritania	205,400	532,000
Morocco	31,660	82,000
Tunisia	27,000	70,000

Glossary

adapt to change in order to suit the conditions

ancestor person who lived long ago from whom someone is descended

barren having such poor soil that no plants grow

boomerang curved piece of wood that can be thrown so that it returns to the thrower

butte flat-topped, steep-sided desert hill; a small mesa

canyon deep, steep-sided valley

caravan group of traders traveling together across a desert, usually with animals such as camels

climate weather conditions in a particular area

continent one of the world's seven huge land masses

current strong, steady flow of water in one direction

date palm tall palm tree on which dates grow as fruit

dew tiny drops of water that form on cool surfaces at night

drought long period of very little rainfall

equator imaginary line that stretches around the middle of Earth

erg area of shifting sand dunes

erosion wearing away (especially of rocks)

exports goods that are sent for sale to another country

famine extreme shortage of food, causing widespread hunger

fertile having rich soil and producing good crops

fiber threadlike substance in a plant

hamada raised area of rocky land

hunter-gatherer wandering person who lives by hunting, fishing and collecting wild food such as roots and berries

irrigate to water land, especially using pipes, canals, and ditches

landscape natural scenery

latitude imaginary lines that stretch around Earth above or below the equator

merchant trader; somebody who buys and sells goods

mesa flat-topped, steep-sided mountain or area of highland in a desert

mineral natural solid substance that is found under Earth's surface

moisture small amount of water; dampness

nomad person who wanders from place to place to find food and grazing land

oasis area in a desert with water where plants can grow

pedestal desert rock that has been worn away into a mushroom shape

pinnacle tall, pointed piece of rock

pioneer someone who goes to an unknown place to explore and possibly to settle there

plateau flat area of high land

polar near the North Pole (in the Arctic region) or the South Pole (in Antarctica)

pore tiny opening

precipitation rain, snow, sleet, or hail that falls to the ground

predator animal that hunts and kills other animals for food

prey animal that is hunted by another animal for food

rain forest thick forest found in warm tropical areas of heavy rainfall

reg flat, stony plain

salt flats area of flat land covered with a layer of salt

sand dune mound or hill of sand formed by the wind

scour to rub hard

species particular kind of animal or plant

tropical having to do with the region of the tropics

tropics hottest region of Earth, between two imaginary lines that stretch around Earth. The tropic of Cancer is above the equator and the tropic of Capricorn is below it.

wadi dry river valley

wind turbine large windmill that powers generators, producing electricity

Further Reading

Chambers, Catherine. *Mapping Earthforms: Deserts*. Chicago: Heinemann Library, 2000.

Lalley, Patrick. *Desert Scientists*. Chicago: Raintree, 2001.

Royston, Angela. *Extreme Survival: Deserts*. Chicago: Raintree, 2003.

Index